To Marguerite, Annabelle and Milan

EGMONT

We bring stories to life

Originally published 2018.
This edition published 2020 by Egmont Limited,
2 Minster Court, 10th Floor, London EC3R 7BB
www.egmont.co.uk

Text and illustrations copyright © Barroux 2018
Barroux has asserted his moral rights.

ISBN 978 0 6035 7919 6

70912/001

Printed in Malaysia

A CIP catalogue record for this book is available from the British Library.

How Many TREES?

BARROUX

EGMONT

How many trees
make a forest?

I know!

I know!

1,500 trees!

I know because I am the **king** of the forest.

You know **nothing!** I know
how many trees make a forest . . .

500 trees!

My favourite tree is an **oak** tree.

No, maybe an **olive** tree.   .

Hmmm,

I like

lemon trees too . . .

I am the **king,** so I decide which tree is the best!

No, you **don't!** And I've changed my mind – my favourite is an apple tree.

You both know nothing!
I know how many trees
make a forest . . .

Me!
Me! I know!

85 trees!

That's enough to
play hide-and-seek
in the **shadows.**

I am the king, so I know best!
It's 1,500 trees!

No, it's 500 trees!

Does anyone want to
play hide-and-seek?

You are all **wrong!**

I know how many trees
make a forest . . .

Hello?
I said I know . . .

40 trees!

That's enough to **hide** from the Hunter!

Or maybe 60 trees is better?

Hmmm,

the Hunter is clever,

so I think 80 trees.

The forest is my kingdom.
I decide everything!

No, you don't!

You are too small
to play hide-and-seek.

How rude! I am very good
at hiding. The Hunter
has never found me!

Excuse me, I know
how many trees
make a forest . . .

No, I know!

Four trees!

One for spring.

One for summer.

One for autumn.

One for winter.

The answer is **one tree** makes a forest.

Because even the **biggest forest** starts with a seed from **one tree.**

Amazing!

Wow!

Ant, you are clever enough
to be king! (For one day.)

Seeds are my favourite things!

I didn't know that!

I love this trees
and seeds story.

Me too, but what came first?
The seed or the tree?